LITTLE RACCOON WHO COULD

Written by Susan Cornell Poskanzer
Illustrated by Susan Hall

Troll Associates

Library of Congress Cataloging in Publication Data

Poskanzer, Susan Cornell.
    Little raccoon who could.

    Summary: Wally Raccoon worries about making his
first trip to school alone as he examines all the
possible pitfalls.
    [1. Schools—Fiction. 2. Raccoons—Fiction]
I. Hall, Susan, 1940-   ill.   II. Title.
PZ7.P8382Li   1986   [E]   85-14020
ISBN 0-8167-0624-7 (lib. bdg.)
ISBN 0-8167-0625-5 (pbk.)

10   9   8   7   6   5   4   3

LITTLE RACCOON
WHO COULD

Wally Raccoon looked worried.

5

"You can do it. I know you
can," said Wally's mother. "You
are getting big. You can walk to
school by yourself. And you can
walk home."

Mrs. Raccoon always walked
Wally to school. Many of
Wally's friends already walked
to school by themselves. But
Wally was afraid. Maybe he was
not old enough yet. Maybe he
would get lost.

"What if I get lost?" asked
Wally.
"You will not get lost," said
Mrs. Raccoon. "You will go the
way we always go. You will
pack your backpack. You will
take your lunch. Then we will
wave goodbye to each other.

"You will go over the bridge.
You will march through the
woods. You will walk around
the pond. You will hike up the
hill. You will skip down the hill.
Then you will be at school.
You can do it, Wally. I know
you can."

"I don't know," said Wally.
"What if the bridge breaks when
I walk over it? There might be
big sharks in the water! I am
afraid of sharks, Mom."

"Dear Wally!" said Mrs. Raccoon. "The bridge is strong. It will not break. No sharks live in the water. You can walk to school by yourself—and home again, too. I know you can."

"I don't know, Mom. What if I
march through the woods and I
see a mushroom? What if I eat
it? What if it makes me sick?
You may never see me again,
Mom," said Wally.

12

"You will not eat anything in the woods. I *will* see you again," said his mother.

"Maybe, Mom," said Wally.
"But what if I walk around the
pond and it starts to rain? And
then the sun comes out.

"And I see a rainbow. I might
stop to look at it. I might stop
for a long time. Then I will
be late for school."

"No, Wally," said his mother.
"You will not stop on the way to
school, even if you see a
rainbow. You will keep walking.
You will not be late for school.
You can walk to school by
yourself—and home again, too.
I know you can."

Wally thought again.
"What if I hike up the hill?" he
asked. "And there is a big hole!
What if I don't look where I am
going? What if I fall into the
hole? What if a giant dug the
hole? What if the hole is a
raccoon trap? What then?"

"Wally, Wally," said Mrs.
Raccoon. "You will hike up the
hill. You will look where you
are going. You will not fall into
a hole. No giant lives on the hill
anyway. You can walk to
school. I know you can."

Wally smiled.

"Then I just have to skip down the hill," he said. "And I will be at school."

"That's right," said Wally's mother. "You will be at school."

The next day Wally packed his
backpack. He took his lunch. He
kissed his mother. He waved
goodbye to her.

He went over the bridge. It did
not break. He saw no sharks.

He marched through the woods.
He saw some mushrooms. He
did not eat them.

He walked around the pond.
It did not rain.

He did not see a rainbow. He *did* see some turtles. They looked at Wally. He looked at them—but only for a minute. He did not stop. He did not want to be late for school.

28

He hiked up the hill. He looked
where he was going. He saw
some stones. He saw some small
holes. He did not see any giant
holes. He did not see any
raccoon traps, either.

He skipped down the hill. There
was the school. He walked
inside with his friends, Sam and
Bernice. Wally felt great.

31

He felt good on the way home, too. His mother met him at the bridge. She was happy to see him.

"How was it?" she asked. "How did you like your walk?"

"Great," said Wally. "I want to
do it every day. Every single
day."

"Really?" asked Mrs. Raccoon.
"Are you sure?"
She looked worried.

"But what if it rains?" she
asked.
"I will wear my raincoat," said
Wally. "I can do it, Mom."

36

"Yes," said Mrs. Raccoon. "But what if it snows?"
"I will wear my heavy coat and boots. I will even take a shovel. If *you* want me to," said Wally, "I can do it."

Wally's mother thought.
"What if you get tired?" she
asked.

"I will not get tired, Mom. I'm
young. I'm strong. I will go to
bed extra early. Don't worry. I
can do it. I can walk to school.
And I can walk home every
day," said Wally.

40

Mrs. Raccoon sat down. She
looked at Wally.
"What if you see a stranger?"
she asked. "What if the stranger
asks you to go with him?"
"I do not talk with strangers. I
would not go with him. Mom,
you know that," said Wally.
"Yes, you are right," she said.

"You *would* wear your raincoat
if it rained. You *would* wear
your heavy coat and boots if it
snowed. Please leave your shovel
at home though, dear."
Mrs. Raccoon smiled.
"You would *not* talk to
strangers. You are getting big.
You can walk to school by
yourself," she said.
"And home again, too," added
Wally.

Mrs. Raccoon hugged Wally.
She looked at her son. She felt
proud of him.

Wally looked at his mother. He
felt proud of her.

"Maybe you can walk with me some days," said Wally. "When you have extra time. Or want some fresh air. Just *some* days, of course."

"Of course," said Mrs. Raccoon.

47

Wally had a snack. Then he went to play.
"I knew I could do it," said Wally. "I knew it all along."